AF559680

The Four Avengers Versus The Elephant

Books by Meena Arora Nayak

How the Greedy Crane Was Killed by the Clever Crab: Two Stories from the Panchatantra

The Monkey's Revenge: Two Stories from the Panchatantra

The Rabbit in the Moon: Two Tales from the Panchatantra

The Four Avengers Versus The Elephant

Two Tales from the Panchatantra

Retold by
Meena Arora Nayak

Illustrations by
Apoorva Lalit

ALEPH BOOK COMPANY
An independent publishing firm
promoted by ***Rupa Publications India***

First published in India in 2025
by Aleph Book Company
7/16 Ansari Road, Daryaganj
New Delhi 110 002

ISBN: 978-93-6523-154-0

1 3 5 7 9 10 8 6 4 2

Printed in India

The Tale of the Dimwit Lion and the Wise Hare

In a forest lived a lion called Mandamati (dimwit). He was puffed up with his own strength and took pride in slaying hapless animals. Every day he would go on a rampage, slaughtering numerous deer, boars, bulls, and hares and still be restless for more. The creatures of that forest lived in constant

fear and were sick and tired of the lion's ceaseless and purposeless killing. One day, conferring with each other, they decided on a system that would give them a modicum of peace. Going to Mandamati, they said to him, 'Maharaj, you kill countless animals every day, even though your hunger is appeased with just one kill. Don't you think that's a waste of your food? If you promise not to go on your killing sprees, we ourselves will select an animal every day from different species and send it to you as your prey. That way you won't have to make any effort to procure your food, and we won't live in fear of being randomly slaughtered by you. You are a king; you must observe a king's dharma.

Just as a healthy body gradually
builds
with a fixed daily dose of
nutrients,
a wise king uses the kingdom's
resources
in measured and incremental
amounts
to build a strong kingship.
Just as a lamp's oil burns bit by
bit
to keep the flame lit,
a good king uses people sparingly
to preserve their efficiency.

Also,

a king who looks after his
subjects
acquires heaven in the other
world
and fame and wealth in this
world.

Moreover,

This is the just law of kingship:
The foolish king who
butchers his subjects like goats,
profits only once, and no more.

Rulers who nurture their subjects
with loving care
grow prosperous day by day.

Rulers who afflict their subjects
with suffering
beget their own downfall.'

The animals' advice appealed to Mandamati, and he said to them, 'I'll accept your proposal. But be warned that the day I don't receive my daily meal of one animal, I'll kill all of you.'

Swearing to keep their end of the bargain, the animals returned to the forest, freed from their fear of the lion. From then on, every day, one of them, regardless of his or her age, circumstance, and family commitment, was selected according to species and sent to the lion at his scheduled time of feeding.

One day, it was the turn of a hare. His ears ringing with words of praise and gratitude from the other animals, but his heart heavy with dread, the hare began to trudge to the lion's den. Wishing he could, somehow, escape the lion, he kept thinking of ways he could make that possible. The more he wished and thought, the slower his feet moved. Then, suddenly, he came upon a well. When he looked down into the water and saw his own reflection, an idea began to form in his mind. After that he hurried to Mandamati's den, but, by this time, the lion was raging with hunger and licking his chops, salivating at the thought of killing every single animal in the forest.

The hare warily approached the lion and bowed.

'O evil hare,' thundered the lion, 'in the first place, you are so tiny that eating you will hardly satisfy my hunger, and then you have the audacity to come late. Today, I'll eat you, and tomorrow, I'll go into the forest and kill all the other animals and eat them.'

'Maharaj,' said the hare in a voice that was so shaky, it sounded like a cracked instrument, 'pardon me for being late. But this is neither my fault nor the fault of the other animals. Will you please listen to the reason for my delay?'

'Hurry up and tell me,' the lion roared.

'Before you find yourself a pulp between my jaws.'

'Maharaj, because today the hares were selected for you, the other animals sent five of us, knowing that one of us would not be enough to satisfy you. However, as we five were on our way to you, another lion came out of his cave and accosted us. "Where are you all going?" he asked. "Think of your guardian gods one last time, because I'm going to eat you."

"We're going to our Maharaj, the king of this forest, Mandamati," we told him. "As per our agreement with him, one animal goes to him, voluntarily, every day. Today five of us are going, because we

are small, and our Maharaj has a big appetite."

"Is that right?" he said. "But this forest is mine. I'm the king here. Therefore, you creatures should make an agreement with me and send me an animal every day; not to that Mandamati. Besides, he's a thief. He has robbed me of my forest. Who is he to take an oath from my animals? And if that Mandamati has any problem with this, he should sort it out with me in a show of strength. Go and call him. Leave your four relatives with me as a guarantee, and go and fetch Mandamati. I'll fight him, and whoever wins will eat the five of you."

'So, you see, Maharaj, this is the reason

for my delay. I came as fast as I could to tell you what the other lion said. Please do whatever you think is right.'

'O hare, take me to that thug lion right away. I'll destroy him,' Mandamati thundered, shaking his mane. 'That's the only way my anger will be appeased. It is said,

> A wise king engages in war
> to benefit his kingdom,
> or to save his good name.
> With no chance of a reward
> and no threat of disrespect,
> only a fool would engage
> in a war.'

'You're absolutely right, Maharaj,' the

hare said. 'But I think you should know that that lion lives in a fort. We saw him come out of it when he accosted us. An enemy who is secure in his fort is difficult to subjugate. It is rightly said,

A fort in a war can accomplish
what thousands of elephants
and lakhs of horses cannot.
Just one archer hiding behind
a fort's wall
can kill a hundred enemies
stationed outside it.
The wisdom of a fort is praised
by every master of statecraft.

In bygone days, fearing the danava, Hiranyakashipu, Indra had Vishvakarma build a fort for him, and he was so pleased with it that he gave a boon to all kings on earth: "If you have a fort, you will celebrate victory." Since then, thousands of forts have been built on earth and will continue to be built as long as there are kings, and the kings have enemies.

Just as a serpent without fangs and an elephant without madness can easily be brought under control, so can a king, who is unprotected by a fort.'

'Even if this thug of a lion is hiding in a fort, you must take me to him,' Mandamati roared. 'I'll destroy him in his fort. It is said,

A new disease and a new enemy
must be rooted out without delay.
A disease can sap one's strength,
and the enemy's strength can grow.

One should never underestimate
a rising enemy.
Wise men equate him
to an advancing disease.

An enemy, who was once
weak and easy to defeat
can become powerful,
just like an ailment that once
was negligible can spread
and become fatal.'

'What you say is right, Maharaj. But I want to warn you that the other lion is not weak by any means. In my humble opinion, you shouldn't challenge him without first assessing his strength. People say,

> One who challenges another,
> eager with excitement,
> failing to assess the
> opponent's strength,
> crashes like a kite on fire.

Also,

> By attacking a strong enemy
> without thought and strategy,
> one is sure to lose face
> even if one is powerful;

like an elephant charging
a stronger foe
only to return with broken tusks.'

'Why are you concerned with these matters of an enemy's strength or weakness?' Mandamati asked, irked. 'Stop talking and just take me to my contender.'

'Then follow me, Maharaj,' the hare said and led Mandamati to the well. Halting near the parapet, he turned to the lion and stated, 'No one can withstand your magnificence, Maharaj. Look! Just seeing you from a distance that coward lion has gone to hide in his fort. Come. Step closer. I'll show him to you.'

As Mandamati came close to the

well and looked down, he saw his own reflection and thought it was another lion. When he roared, the sound echoed in the well, and its reverberations were much louder than his own roar. Seeing and hearing his adversary, Mandamati became eager to fight him and jumped into the well. Needless to say, he drowned.

Ecstatic at the lion's demise, the hare ran back to the forest to give the good news to all the other animals. Everyone praised the hare for his brilliant mind and thanked him profusely. From that day on, they all lived happily and in peace.

The Tale of How the Sparrow, Woodpecker, Bee, and Frog Teamed Up to Kill the Elephant

In a forest, on a tamala (bay leaf) tree, there lived a sparrow couple. Once, when the female sparrow had just laid eggs, an intoxicated, wild elephant, exhausted and sweating from the heat, came and stood under the tree. In his madness, he wrapped his trunk around the branch on which the sparrows were nesting and broke it. All the eggs fell on the ground and smashed, but the sparrow couple, somehow, survived. The bereaved mother sparrow was beside herself with grief and spent all day weeping and lamenting. Her friend, the woodpecker, who had seen the tragedy, could hardly bear her heart-wrenching sobs and tried to console her. 'Hush, my friend. Stop crying,' he said. 'Your tears won't bring your babies back. The wise say,

People who are able to think
logically

do not bemoan the past, the lost,
and the dead.
This is how an intelligent one
differs from a fool.

Besides,

All creatures in this world
are mortal and evanescent.
It is foolish to weep for them.
Grieving for the perishable,
one sinks deeper into grief.

Also, think about this:

The spirits of the departed
drink the tears of the bereaved,
It is not tears the departed need
but death rites and rituals

to benefit the soul's afterlife.'

'You're right, dear friend,' the sparrow said to the woodpecker. 'But how can I forgive this wicked elephant who destroyed our offspring in a fit of madness? If you consider yourself my friend, help me avenge my loss. Only by killing this elephant will I feel consoled and find peace.'

'I know what you mean,' said the woodpecker.

'A true friend comes to your aid
in times of need.
Everyone can be your friend in
times of prosperity.

Need is what brings people
together,
not caste or race similarities.

It is also said:

A friend who helps in need
is a true friend indeed.
A son who is devoted to
his parents is a true son indeed.
A servant who fulfils his duty
is a true servant indeed.
A wife whose husband is happy
is a true wife indeed.

Now watch me. See how I punish that elephant who killed your children. I'll enlist the help of my friend, the bee, Veenarava (hum of a veena).'

Then, the woodpecker took the sparrow with him to meet the bee. 'This is my friend, Sparrow,' he said to Veenarava. 'A wild, mad elephant smashed her eggs on the ground and didn't even apologize. She's feeling outraged and very dejected. Can you help us punish that elephant?'

'Need you even ask?' Veenarava said. 'Your friend is dearer to me than even you, because it is said,

Friends helping friends is merely
a give and take of friendship.
But to help a friend's friend—
now that is true friendship.

But wait, I, too, have a friend—a frog. His name is Meghanada (music of

the clouds). Let me call him as well. Together, we'll come up with the best strategy to destroy that wicked elephant. As they say,

The remedy one concocts together
with educated and wise friends,
who are well-wishers and
well-intentioned,
is often flawless and apt,
and it never fails to be effective.'

Hence, the three of them—the sparrow, the woodpecker, and the bee went to meet Meghanada, the frog, and told him the whole story.

'That intoxicated elephant will be reduced to nothing by our combined effort,' the frog promised. 'Here is what I suggest: Bee, go and gently buzz in the elephant's ear. Hearing your sweet hum, he'll get drowsy and close his eyes. Woodpecker, after that, it'll be your turn. Once the elephant goes to sleep, you'll peck his eyes out and blind him. When he awakens, he'll be thirsty, but being blind, he won't know where to go. I'll then go to a dark pit and begin croaking. Following my frog sound, thinking it must be from a nearby pond, he'll stagger towards me and, inevitably, tumble into the pit and die. In this way, we'll form a group of avengers and avenge the death of Sparrow's babies.'

The four avengers then followed the plan: Veenarava, the bee, flew to the elephant and began to hum a lullaby in his ear. As soon as he fell asleep, the woodpecker poked his eyes out with his beak. When the elephant woke up and began lurching around, looking for water, Meghanada, the frog, found a deep pit and began croaking from its edge. Following that siren sound, the elephant tumbled into the pit and died.